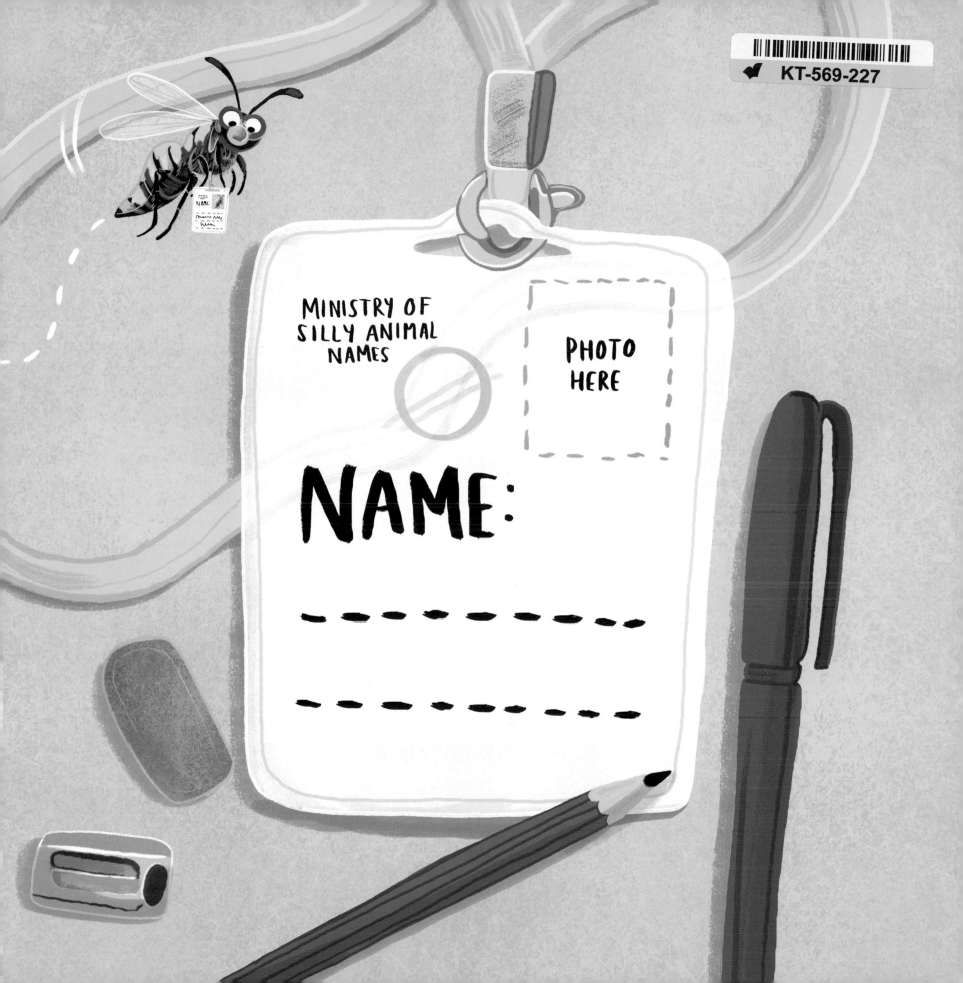

To Dylan, Faith, Megan
and . . . DAVE! – K.G.

For Lucy and Alice,
with love. x – N.D.

First published 2018 by Macmillan Children's Books
an imprint of Pan Macmillan
This edition published 2019 by Macmillan Children's Books
20 New Wharf Road, London N1 9RR
Associated companies throughout the world
www.panmacmillan.com

ISBN: 978-1-5290-2320-6

Text copyright © Kes Gray 2018
Illustration copyright © Nikki Dyson 2018

Kes Gray and Nikki Dyson have asserted their rights to be identified
as the author and illustrator of this work in accordance with the
Copyright, Designs and Patents Act 1988.

Pages 30-31 Photographs © Shutterstock
Additional photographs: Bone-Eating Snot Flower Worm © Alamy /
the Natural History Museum; Pink Fairy Armadillo © FLPA; Blobfish
© Caters News Agency; Ice Cream Cone Worm © Hans Hillewaert;
Monkeyface Prickleback: NOAA/MBARI

9 8 7 6 5 4 3 2 1

A CIP catalogue record for this book is
available from the British Library.

Printed in China

"YOU'RE CALLED WHAT?!"

KES GRAY + NIKKI DYSON

MACMILLAN CHILDREN'S BOOKS

It was another busy day at the Ministry of Silly Animal Names.

"I'd like to change my name, please," said the dog who was next in the queue.

"May I ask why?" said the Secretary Bird behind the counter.

"Because I'm a Cockapoo," said the Cockapoo.

"HA HA HA HA!" laughed all the other animals with silly names.

MINISTRY
OF SILLY
ANIMAL NAMES
NAME:
COCKAPOO

"You see," said the Cockapoo,
"whenever I say what sort of dog
I am, everybody laughs."

"I'd rather be a Cockapoo than a Monkeyface Prickleback," said the Monkeyface Prickleback standing at window number two.

"**HA HA HA HA HA!**" laughed all the other animals with silly names.
"That can't be a real name for an animal."
"It is," sighed the Monkeyface Prickleback.

"I'd rather be a Monkeyface Prickleback than a Pink Fairy Armadillo," sighed the Pink Fairy Armadillo at window number three.

"HA HA HA HA HA HA!" laughed all the other animals with silly names.

"At least you're not a Blue-Footed Booby," said the Blue-Footed Booby at window number four.

"HA HA HA HA HA HA HA!" laughed all the other animals with silly names.

"At least you're not an Ice Cream Cone Worm," sighed the Ice Cream Cone Worm at window number five.

"At least you're not a Shovelnose Guitarfish!" said the Shovelnose Guitarfish standing at window number six.

"HA HA HA HA HA HA HA HA HA HA HA!" laughed all the other animals with silly names.

MINISTRY OF SILLY ANIMAL NAMES
NAME: BLUE-FOOTED BOOBY
NAME: PINK FAIRY ARMADILLO
NAME: ICE CREAM CONE
MINISTRY OF SILLY ANIMAL NAMES
NAME: SHOVELNOSE GUITARFISH

“Imagine being called a BLOBFISH,” sighed the Blobfish at window number seven.

“HA HA HA HA HA HA HA HA HA HA HA HA HA HA HA HA!”

laughed all the other animals with silly names.

"I mean, it's not as if I look like a blob, is it?!"

"AHEM," went all the other animals with silly names.

"I don't exactly look like a Bone-Eating Snot Flower Worm, do I?"
said the Bone-Eating Snot Flower Worm at window number eight.
"But it didn't stop me being called one."

"HA HA HA HA HA HA HA HA HA HA HA HA HA HA HA HA!"
laughed all the other animals with silly names.

"I'll give you a million guesses what I got called," frowned the fish at window number nine.

"A Fungus Faced Flounder?" guessed the Monkeyface Prickleback.

"A Gungy Gobbed Grouper?" guessed the Pink Fairy Armadillo.

"Tell us!" said the Blue-Footed Booby.

"Yes, tell us," said the Bone-Eating Snot Flower Worm. "We promise not to laugh."

"A Tasselled Wobbegong," sighed the Tasselled Wobbegong.

"HA HA HA HA HA HA HA HA HA HA HA HA HA HA HA HA!"
laughed all the other animals with silly names.
"YOU'RE CALLED WHAT?!"

"I thought being a Winkle sounded silly!" said the Winkle at window number ten.

"I thought being a Fried Egg Jellyfish sounded silly," said the Fried Egg Jellyfish at window number eleven. "But a TASSELLED WOBBEGONG? No wonder everyone is laughing!"

"Get ready to laugh some more," sighed the wasp at window number twelve.

"My name is so silly,
it's impossible to say it
WITHOUT laughing."

"What kind of wasp are you then?" asked the Fried Egg Jellyfish.

MINISTRY
OF
SILLY ANIMAL
NAMES
NAME:
FRIED
EGG
JELLYFISH

"I'm an Aha Ha,"
said the wasp.

"AHA HA HA HA HA!"
laughed all the other animals with silly names.

"No, an AHA HA," frowned the wasp.

"AHA AHA AHA AHA AHA AHA!" laughed all the other animals with silly names.

"NO. Not an AHA AHA AHA AHA AHA
AHA," insisted the wasp.
"An AHA HA!"

"AHA HA HA HA HA HA HA HA HA HA HA HA HA HA HA HA HA
HA HA HA HA HA HA HA HA HA HA HA HA HA HA HA HA!"
laughed all the other animals with silly names.

"Right, that's it," fumed the Aha Ha. "I'd like to change my name immediately, please."

"Of course," said the Secretary Bird at window number twelve.
"And what would you like your new name to be?"

FACTS AND SNAPS!

Name: Blue-Footed Booby
Wingspan: 81-86 cm
Fact: Found in the Galapagos Islands, male blue-footed boobies dance to attract females and the bluer their feet, the better. Boogie, booby!

Name: Secretary Bird
Height: 90-137 cm
Fact: Named for its crest of quill-like feathers, this predator is great at catching snakes. Eek!

Name: Tasselled Wobbegong
Size: 117-125 cm
Fact: Found in coral reefs, these sharks have several rows of sharp, fang-like teeth. Yikes!

Name: Winkle
Average Size: 3.8 cm
Fact: These creatures are typically eaten with vinegar by humans in the coastal areas of the UK. Yum!

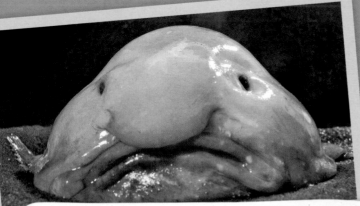

Name: Blobfish
Average Size: 30 cm
Fact: Voted the world's ugliest animal, the Blobfish lives in deep ocean waters and has no muscles. Floppy as well as blobby.

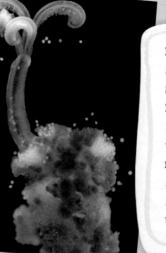

Name: Bone-Eating Snot Flower Worm
Size: 1-2 cm
Fact: Discovered in California, this worm has no mouth or gut — so it absorbs bone material that it's dissolved with its roots using acid. Yuck!

Name: Fried Egg Jellyfish
Average Size: 35 cm
Fact: This Mediterranean jellyfish has a very weak sting. Chips with this, anyone?

Name: Aha Ha Wasp
Average Size: 30 mm
Fact: The Aha Ha Wasp was named by the entomologist Arnold Menke in 1977 as a joke. This wasp is so reclusive, we couldn't find a photo of him!

Name: Shovelnose Guitarfish
Length: Up to 1.7 m
Fact: Usually found in the Gulf of California, this ray, unlike most rays, doesn't have any barbs or stingers so it's harmless to humans. Let's play!

Name: Monkeyface Prickleback
Average Size: 76 cm
Fact: Found on the Pacific coast of North America, these fish have long, eel-shaped bodies and always look surprised. Why?

Name: Pink Fairy Armadillo
Size: 9–11.5 cm
Fact: Found mainly in Central Argentina, these creatures are excellent diggers and can completely bury themselves in a matter of seconds if threatened. Hide and seek, everybody!

Name: Cockapoo
Size: 25–38 cm
Fact: This friendly pup is a cross between a Cocker Spaniel and a Poodle and is super energetic. Adorable!

Name: Ice Cream Cone Worm
Size: 4–6 cm
Fact: Found in North America, their tiny, cone-shaped shells are made of a single layer of sand grains and bits of other shell, all glued together. Delicious!